Dear Parent:

Your child's love of reading starts here!

Every child learns to read in a different way and at his or her own speed. You can help your young reader improve and become more confident by encouraging his or her own interests and abilities. You can also guide your child's spiritual development by reading stories with biblical values and Bible stories, like I Can Read! books published by Zonderkidz. From books your child reads with you to the first books he or she reads alone, there are I Can Read! books for every stage of reading:

SHARED READING
Basic language, word repetition, and whimsical illustrations, ideal for sharing with your emergent reader.

BEGINNING READING
Short sentences, familiar words, and simple concepts for children eager to read on their own.

READING WITH HELP
Engaging stories, longer sentences, and language play for developing readers.

READING ALONE
Complex plots, challenging vocabulary, and high-interest topics for the independent reader.

ADVANCED READING
Short paragraphs, chapters, and exciting themes for the perfect bridge to chapter books.

I Can Read! books have introduced children to the joy of reading since 1957. Featuring award-winning authors and illustrators and a fabulous cast of beloved characters, I Can Read! books set the standard for beginning readers.

A lifetime of discovery begins with the magical words "I Can Read!"

Visit www.icanread.com for information on enriching your child's reading experience.
Visit www.zonderkidz.com for more Zonderkidz I Can Read! titles.

You each have your own gift from God.
One has this gift. Another has that.
—*1 Corinthians 7:7*

To Maddie, the original tea-party girl.
—*S.H.*

ZONDERKIDZ

Howie's Tea Party
Copyright © 2008 by Sara Henderson
Illustrations copyright © 2008 by Aaron Zenz

Requests for information should be addressed to:
Zonderkidz, Grand Rapids, Michigan 49530

Library of Congress Cataloging-in-Publication Data

Henderson, Sara, 1952-
    Howie's tea party / story by Sara Henderson ; pictures by Aaron Zenz.
        p. cm. — (I can read! My first level)
    Summary: Emma tries her best to turn her puppy, Howie, into Mrs. Brown,
    a proper tea party guest.
    ISBN 978-0-310-71605-1 (softcover)
    1. Afternoon teas—Fiction. 2. Dogs—Fiction. 3. Animals—Infancy—Fiction.
    4. Christian life—Fiction. I. Zenz, Aaron, ill. II. Title.
    PZ7.H3835Hox 2008
    [E]—dc22
                                                                2007034317

Editor: Betsy Flikkema
Art direction: Jody Langley
Cover design: Sarah Molegraaf

Printed in China

10 11 12 13 SCC 6 5 4 3

ZONDER**kidz**

I Can Read!

SHARED

My First

READING

HOWiE's TEA PARTY

story by Sara Henderson

pictures by Aaron Zenz

Howie, do you want some tea?

Come, Howie, come.

Let's play tea party.

Here is a hat for you to put on.

You can be Mrs. Brown.

Mrs. Brown,

how nice you came for tea.

Please sit down
and talk with me.

We'll have some tea.

It will be so much fun.

But dear Mrs. Brown,

please come to the table!

Do you see the cookies?

They're your favorite kind.

If you come to the table,

you may have one or two.

The party is not under there.
Mrs. Brown, please come out!

Wait! Wait! Wait!
We haven't had tea.

Howie, I mean Mrs. Brown,
come back here!

Stop, Howie, stop!

Do not lick the food!

I mean, Mrs. Brown,
where are your manners?

No, Howie, no!

Stop running around.

I'll pour the tea
if you'll just sit down.

Howie, come here.

You must do as I say.

I mean, Mrs. Brown,
please take your seat!

This is not how we play.
Howie, I mean Mrs. Brown,
get off!

No, Howie, no!

Don't pull the tablecloth!

28

Howie, Howie,
just look at this mess.
You ruined my party!

Mrs. Brown, you look so sad.

I mean, Howie,

I'm sorry I yelled at you.

God made you to run and play.
That's what puppies do.

God made you just as you are.

I'm glad you're my Howie,

and not Mrs. Brown.